See, Hear, Feel

MINDFULNESS FOR CHILDREN – ONE MOMENT AT A TIME

Emmanuelle Giumelli

Illustrated by Mathilde Gatinois
Designed by Patricia Murphey

Wisdom

To Tom, Raphael & Delphine, and
the children who inspire my life daily.
— Emmanuelle

To Ulysse, Léo, Etienne & Arièle
— Mathilde

To Rodrigo, Diego & Bella
— Patricia

Hi, I am Charlie.

I like to see, hear, and feel my day.
It makes me happy.
Come see, hear, and feel my day with me.

I open my eyes to a brand-new day.

I see the morning sunlight.
I hear familiar voices.
I feel the softness of Squeaky, my mouse.

I open the jelly jar.

I see yummy red goodness.
I hear more toast popping up.
I feel sticky.

I open the toothpaste.

I see my face in the mirror.
I hear *brush, brush.*
I feel foamy bubbles.

I open the bag of dog food.

I see Juno wagging his tail.
I hear *woof, woof.*
I feel proud Juno is my dog.

I open my hand on my belly.

I see myself become still.
I hear my breath go in and out.
I feel my belly go up and down.

I open the window.

I see trees, people, a train.
I hear music - my voice singing.
I feel sleepy, excited, and curious.

I open my classroom door.

I see my friends and my teacher.
I hear talking, laughing, playing.
I feel eager to play but sad to see my mom go.

I open the gate when school is done.

I see children everywhere.
I hear "Goodbye, see you tomorrow!"
I feel happy to go home.

I open my hawk eyes.

I see small smooth rocks and a big lumpy one.
I hear bird songs.
I feel playful.

I open my ears to play the listening game.

I hear the train far away, the wind nearby,
and my breath inside my body.
I see a big tree.
I feel calm and focused.

I open my mouth wide.

I see the colors and shapes of
the food on the table.
I hear *slurp, slurp.*
I feel hungry in my belly.

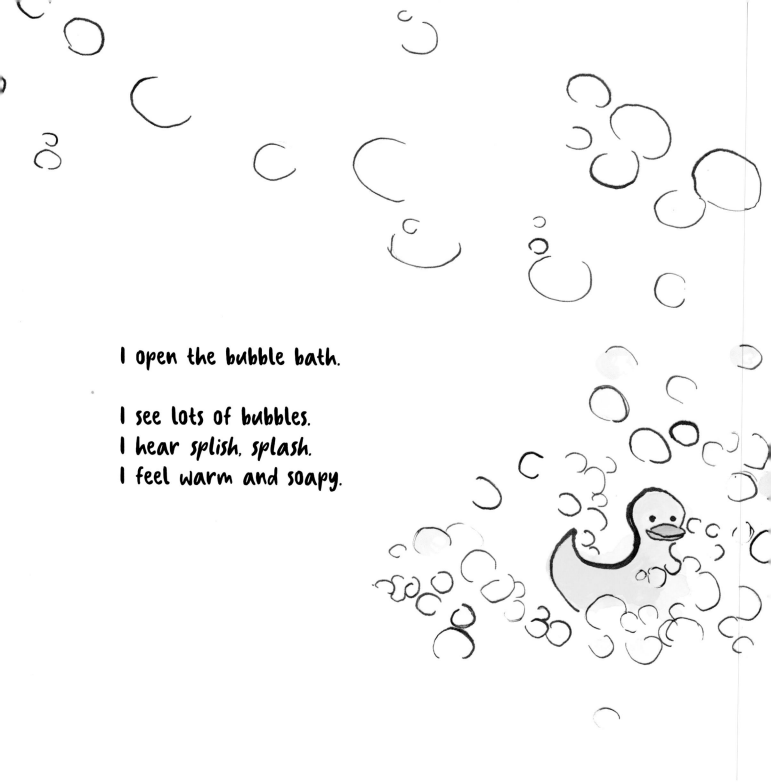

I open the bubble bath.

I see lots of bubbles.
I hear *splish, splash.*
I feel warm and soapy.

I open my arms to snuggle with my dad.

I see his smile.
I hear "Good night, I love you"
and whispered words.
I feel loved and safe.

I close my eyes and send my teacher love and kindness.

In my head, I see my teacher smiling.
I hear my voice: "Be happy; have sweet dreams."
I feel joy in my heart and sleepy in my body.

I am falling asleep.

I see nothing; my eyes are closed.

I hear quiet noises.

I feel my head on my pillow, my back and legs touching the bed, and Squeaky on my belly going up and down.

MINDFULNESS
ACTIVITIES
AND GAMES

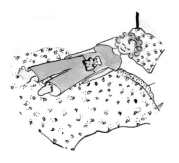

See, Hear, Feel illustrates mindfulness in a way your child can relate to, enabling him or her to develop a frame of reference for the experiences the book depicts. Thus, through reading the story about Charlie, your child will develop familiarity with mindfulness of daily activities. This should help support your introduction to your child of the following mindfulness practices of seeing, hearing, and feeling.

Your child may not always respond in a calm and focused manner while exploring the following activities. Take a moment to notice your motivations and expectations in introducing mindfulness to your child. Keep activity time short, and let your child guide you.

MINDFUL BREATHING

Mindful breathing is bringing our awareness to the breath.

Through this practice children are able to develop awareness of the movement of the breath in their body. This will help them to increase their awareness of the sensations of different emotions and notice what their experience is in those moments. Mindful breathing also teaches children how to self-regulate, which gives them a sense of control. Most children express that they experience a sense of calm and peacefulness during or after mindful breathing.

Keep in mind that some children may be resistant to mindful breathing at first; if this is the case with your child, start with activities such as mindful hearing, feeling, or eating.

ROCKING YOUR ANIMAL TO SLEEP

After having your child lie down, put a stuffed animal on the child's belly, and ask the child to rock the animal to sleep using their breath. Remind the child to breathe normally and to notice their belly going up and down. The child can also put their hands on their belly. This is a great activity to do before bedtime.

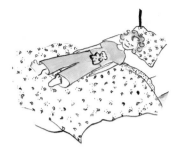

MINDFUL FEELING

THE BODY SCAN

The body scan activity will develop children's sensory awareness. Your child can lie on his or her back or sit on a chair with feet flat on the ground. Invite your child to notice sensations on and in his or her body. Say something like the following:

"Put your hands on your belly and take a deep breath in and out. Do you notice your belly going up and down? Now take a regular breath. Do you still notice your belly going up and down?

"Wiggle your toes. Can you feel your sock? Can you feel your feet moving? What does it feel like?

"Can you feel your legs touching the floor? Does it feel hard or soft? Cold or warm? Do you feel your clothes touching the skin on your legs? Do your legs feel heavy or light?

"Can you feel your back touching the floor? Does it feel hard or soft? Cold or warm?

"Now bring your attention to your belly. Notice your belly going up and down with each breath. Notice your chest; is it also going up and down with your breath?

"Put your hand on top of your heart. You may be able to feel your heartbeat, but you have to be really, really quiet to feel it."

Continue throughout your child's body. Invite your child to notice sensations on his or her back, arms, hands, face, and head, and then guide your child back to the breath.

THE BODY SCAN VARIATION

Sometimes introducing touch to the body scan can enhance the sensations; this can make it easier for children to notice them. However, some children can be sensitive to being touched, so you might want to ask permission first.

Say something like the following: "We are going to do a body scan, and if it's okay with you, I will gently squeeze and release to help you notice my hand on your body."

If the child says it's okay, place your hand lightly on the child's arm, squeeze a little, and then release. Do the same with his or her hand, other arm, other hand, leg, foot, other leg, and other foot.

If the child seems uncomfortable, try the regular body scan on the previous page.

HEARTFULNESS

Generosity, gratitude, love, and kindness are a part of mindfulness called *heartfulness*. Practicing such qualities helps develop caring, empathy, and kindness in children.

These are everyday activities to send love and kindness to ourselves, the people in our lives, our communities, and beyond.

LOVE AND KINDNESS TO OTHERS

Say something like the following: "Think about someone you love, maybe someone you see every day. It can be a person, a pet, anything. Imagine that person smiling, or your pet wagging its tail. Let's fill our hearts with love and kindness for them and send them our wishes:

> 'I wish you to be happy.
> I wish you to be healthy.
> I wish you to be safe.'

"And now make up your own wishes.

"All the love and kindness is reaching and showering that person or pet. They are feeling so happy. Notice how it feels in your own body when you send love and kind wishes."

LOVE AND KINDNESS TO SELF

This activity familiarizes children with how to be kind to themselves and also helps them develop an awareness and a sensory experience of what love and kindness feel like in their body.

"In your mind, see yourself with a smile on your face doing something you love. This time we are going to send love and kindness to ourselves. Let's fill our hearts with love and kindness, and send those wishes to ourselves:

'May I be happy.
May I be healthy.
May I be safe.'

"And now make up your own wish for yourself.

"Notice how it feels in your own body when you send yourself love and kindness."

MINDFUL EATING

This is a fun activity to share and have tons of fun with during family meals or snack times.

"Pick an item from your plate and look at its texture, color, and shape.

"What does it look like? Smell like?

"Put it in your mouth and chew slowly. What do you notice first? What do you notice as you keep chewing?"

MINDFUL LISTENING: FAR, NEAR, INSIDE GAME

You can play this game indoors or outdoors. Have your child draw or write down all the sounds he or she hears and then move on to the next question. You can also stop and share what you heard before moving on.

"What sounds can you hear that are really far away?

"What sounds can you hear that are near? Loud sounds and quiet sounds?

"What sounds can you hear inside your body? Your breath, your belly grumbling?"

MINDFUL SEEING: ANIMAL EYES GAME

Ask your child what animals have great sight. Act out different animals.

Tell the child to put on their hawk eyes (or whatever animal your child chooses to be) and find the following:

Something big, small, really tiny.
Something beautiful.
Something peaceful.
Something out of place.

PUTTING IT ALL TOGETHER: THE SEEING, LISTENING, FEELING GAME

In the car, on a walk, or while you wait:

Identify what you see, such as branches moving, people, or dogs. Or play the Animal Eyes Game.

Identify what you hear, or play Far, Near, Inside.

Identify what you feel. This can be sensory, such as the rocks under your feet or the feeling of shade, sun, or wind on your body; or it can be emotions, such as happy, curious, or frustrated.

MAKE A MIND JAR

The mind jar can represent our own brain. When we shake the jar the glitter goes all over, reminding us of when we are very excited, hyper, overwhelmed, sad, angry, and so on. Then the glitter settles to the bottom of the jar. Using the mindfulness activities in this book can help your brain settle and find calm and peace. It can help us settle our glitter! Mindfulness can help us notice that our brain is activated, and we can use mindfulness activities to help us change the experience in our brain and body.

You will need:

One small mason jar
Glitter glue
Glitter
Hot water

Steps:

Pour the hot water into the jar.
Add the glitter glue and stir until dissolved.
Add glitter.
Put the lid back on.
Shake the jar and watch the glitter dance and settle.

COLOR YOUR MIND JARS

DRAW A PICTURE OF YOURSELF DOING ONE OF THE ACTIVITIES

AUTHOR'S NOTE

Mindfulness means paying attention to your experience, or noticing things on purpose. We can be mindful of everything, including sound, sight, smell, taste, touch, and our thoughts and emotions. The misconception that *mindfulness* means sitting still and being calm may make you wonder how in the world kids can do that!

See, Hear, Feel offers ways to introduce mindfulness to children, illustrating what a mindful day can look like and how you can incorporate mindfulness into your children's daily lives without it seeming like yet another thing they have to do. The practice of mindfulness will give your children tools to self-regulate and self-soothe. It will develop their self-awareness and give them a moment to pause and reflect on their actions and relationships.

In writing *See, Hear, Feel*, I sought to create a book that children and parents can enjoy together, and that might provide them with a means to connect. In talking with parents and children, I found that what appears to be most important to them is that they feel a deep connection to each other. Often we are physically present with our children but our mind is in the past or the future. Clearly, we cannot be present every moment of the day, but when we are fully present or attuned as parents, we are mindful, and that can guide our children to have the experience of what it feels like to be in the moment. During this attunement between parent and child, the brain activity of the parent affects the brain activity of the child. My wish for you, readers, is for your relationship with your children to overflow with such present-moment awareness. You will find *See, Hear, Feel* useful whether you are just getting started on your mindfulness journey or are already on your way.

Go ahead and share this book with the children in your life.

Explore, experiment & have fun!

Emmanuelle Giumelli

Author

Mathilde Gatinois

Illustrator

Patricia Murphey

Graphic Designer

Three friends, one dream.
A lot of love and mindfulness
to make this book a reality.

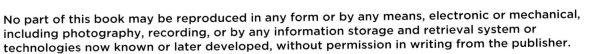

Wisdom Publications
199 Elm Street
Somerville, MA 02144 USA
wisdompubs.org

Library of Congress Cataloging-in-Publication Data
Names: Giumelli, Emmanuelle, author. | Gatinois, Mathilde, illustrator.
Title: See, hear, feel: mindfulness for children, one moment at a time / Emmanuelle Giumelli; illustrated by Mathilde Gatinois.
Description: Somerville, MA: Wisdom Publications, 2018. | Summary: Throughout his day, Charlie finds happiness and comfort by paying attention to sounds, sights, and other sensations. Includes mindfulness activities and games.
Identifiers: LCCN 2018004196 | ISBN 9781614295297 (hardback)
Subjects: | CYAC: Mindfulness (Psychology)—Fiction. | BISAC: JUVENILE FICTION / Social Issues / Emotions & Feelings. | JUVENILE FICTION / Concepts / Senses & Sensation.
Classification: LCC PZ7.1.G584 See 2018 | DDC [E]—dc23
LC record available at https://lccn.loc.gov/2018004196

ISBN 978-1-61429-529-7   ebook ISBN 978-1-61429-551-8

22 21 20 19 18   5 4 3 2 1

Set in Sookie 20/23 and Gotham Medium 11/16.

Wisdom Publications' books are printed on acid-free paper and meet the guidelines for permanence and durability of the Production Guidelines for Book Longevity of the Council on Library Resources.

This book was produced with environmental mindfulness. For more information, please visit wisdompubs.org/wisdom-environment.

Printed in China.